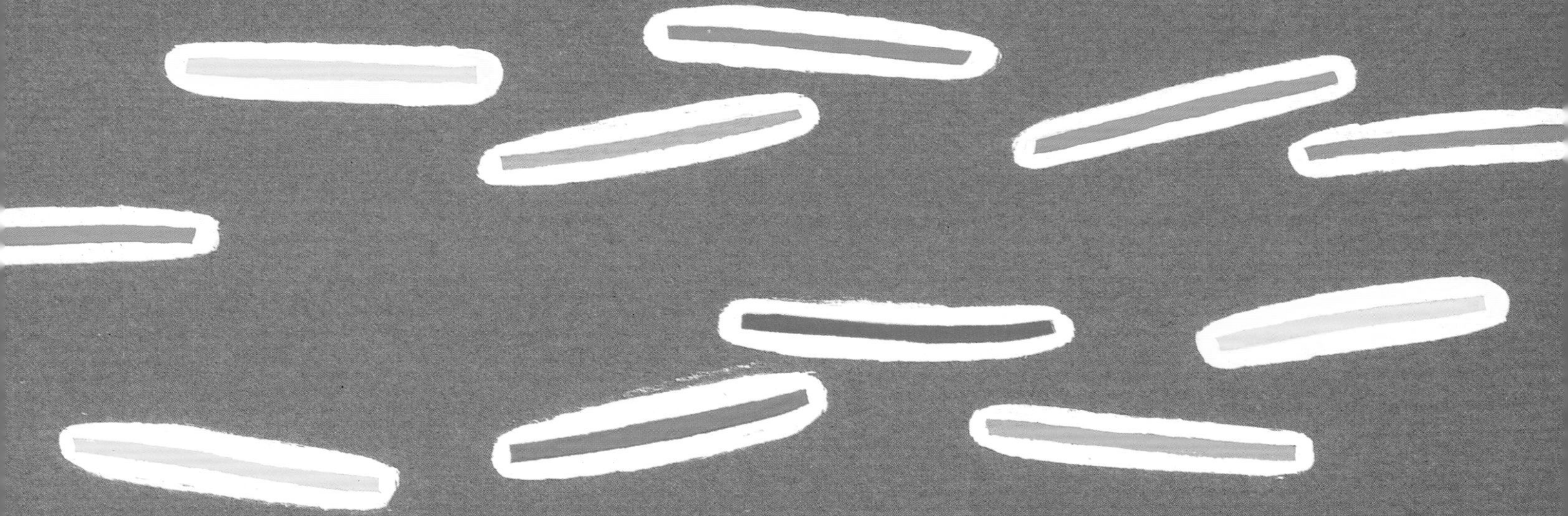

Original title in Galician: **A Cebra Camila**

**books for dreaming** collection

text copyright © 1999 by Marisa Núñez
illustrations copyright © 1999 by Óscar Villán
translation copyright © 2002 by Susana López Rubio

Design by Kalandraka

First published 2002 by Kalandraka Edicions
Av. Josep Tarradellas 118, 1er B
08029 Barcelona
edicions@kalandraka.com
www.kalandraka.com
ISBN: 84.95730.39.1
LD: B.22989.02

# Camilla the zebra

MARISA NÚÑEZ

ÓSCAR VILLÁN

Out there, where the wind roams,
in a country nearest to the end of the world,
lived a little zebra named Camilla.

In that place, the wind was so powerful
that Camilla had to be very careful
not to lose her clothes.

Her mother always advised her
not to go out without her trousers or her suspenders,
but Camilla was growing bigger every day
and the trousers and suspenders
were beginning to be a nuisance.

Camilla daydreamed about lounging in the grass
without all those tight-fitting clothes.
She also imagined that the wind
would blow her away, carrying her through the fields.

One day, Camilla ignored her mother's advice and left her house...

Do you know what happened?

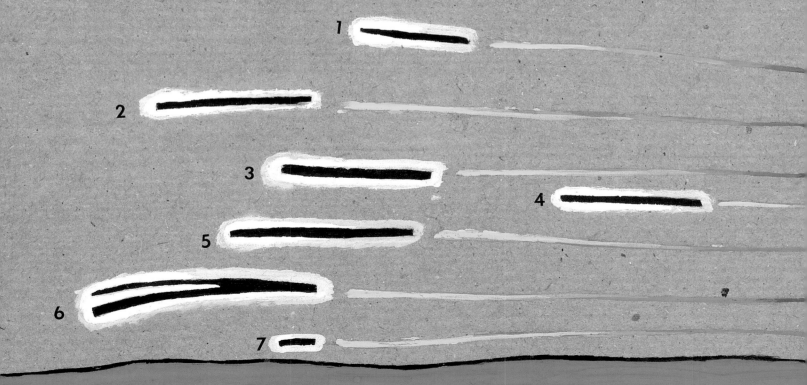

Due to a mighty gust of wind,
she was no longer a striped zebra.
she became something similar to a white mule
wearing a striped t-shirt.

When she saw herself so white and bare,
Camilla started to cry.

Camilla cried SEVEN tears
for her lost stripes.

Afterwards, she stopped to look at a snake
who was shedding her skin.

– Why are you crying? -asked the snake.

– Because a mighty wind blew,
and it took away all my stripes
-she answered, sobbing.

– Come closer. I'll give you a ring
for you to wear on your leg -said the snake

(who appeared to know many secrets).

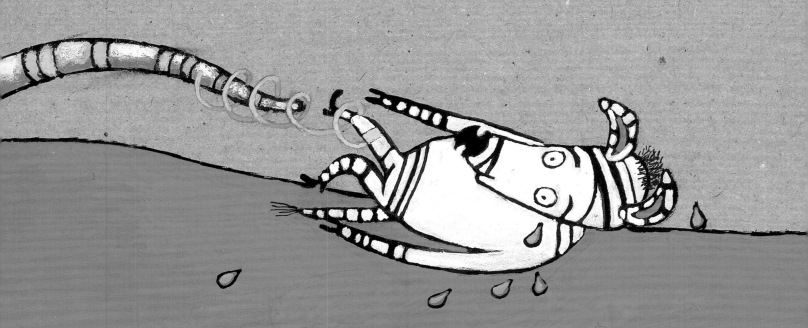

Camilla walked away, wearing the ring
with a much lighter heart.

She cried SIX tears for the stripes she was missing.

Afterwards, she stopped to look at a snail
who was sunbathing because he was very pale.

- Why are you crying? -asked the snail.

- Because a mighty wind blew,
  and it took away all my stripes
  -she answered, sobbing.

- Come closer.
I'll climb up your belly
and stick a silver streak on you.

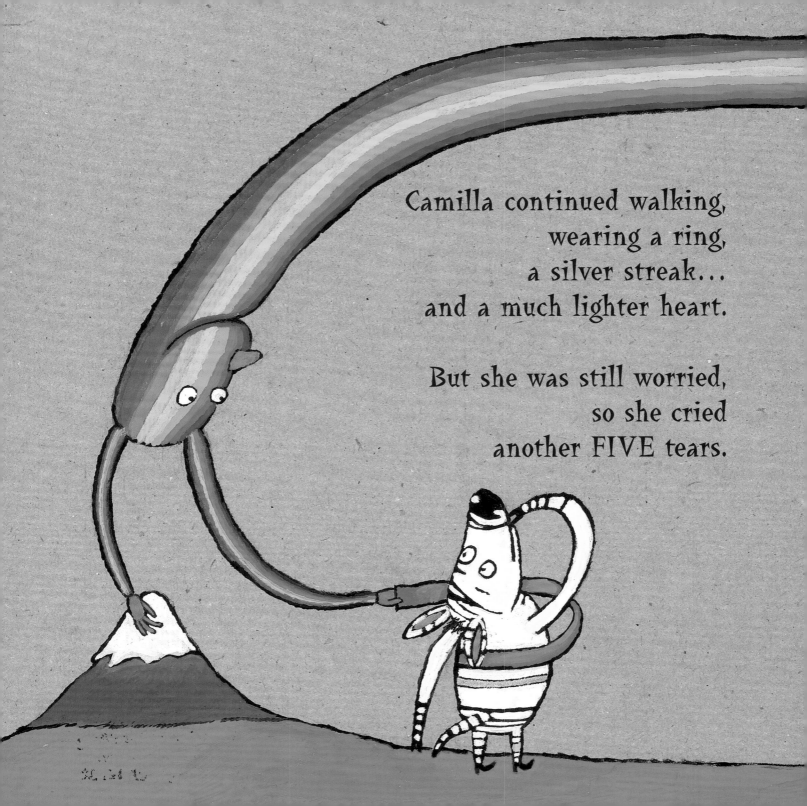

Camilla continued walking,
wearing a ring,
a silver streak...
and a much lighter heart.

But she was still worried,
so she cried
another FIVE tears.

Afterwards, she stopped to look at a rainbow
and stared at it, trying to count all its colors.

– Why are you crying?- asked the rainbow.

– Because a mighty wind blew,
   and it took away all my stripes
   -she answered, sobbing.

– Come closer. I'll hand you a bow made of silk,
   as cool as a beautiful spring morning.

Camilla continued walking,
wearing a ring,
a silver streak
a nice bow made of silk...
and a much lighter heart.

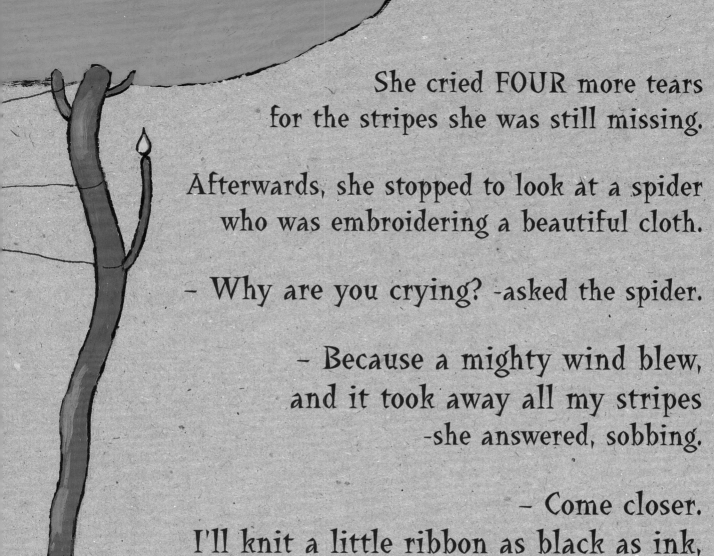

She cried FOUR more tears
for the stripes she was still missing.

Afterwards, she stopped to look at a spider
who was embroidering a beautiful cloth.

– Why are you crying? -asked the spider.

– Because a mighty wind blew,
and it took away all my stripes
-she answered, sobbing.

– Come closer.
I'll knit a little ribbon as black as ink,
which will make you look very elegant.

Camilla continued walking,
wearing a ring, a silver streak,
a nice bow made of silk, a ribbon as black as ink...
and a much lighter heart.

She wept THREE more tears
for the stripes she was still missing.

Afterwards, she stopped to look at a cicada
who was playing a catchy tune.

- Why are you crying? -asked the cicada.

- Because a mighty wind blew,
and it took away all my stripes
-she answered, sobbing.

- Come closer. I'll give you
a string from my violin
so my music can keep you company.

Camilla continued walking,
wearing a ring, a silver streak
a nice bow made of silk, a ribbon as black as ink,
a string from a violin…
and a much lighter heart.

When she was almost home, she cried TWO more tears
for the stripes she was missing.

Afterwards, she stopped to look at a goose
who was limping because one of her boots was too tight.

- Why are you crying? -asked the goose.

- Because a mighty wind blew, and it took away all my stripes -she answered, sobbing.

- Come closer. I'll tie my boot lace to your back and we'll both be much more comfortable.

The goose happily walked away,
after taking off her boot.

Camilla had walked for miles, when, at last,
she arrived home, wearing a ring,
a silver streak, a nice bow made of silk,
a ribbon as black as ink, a string from a violin,
a boot lace fastened with a small pin...
and an almost completely light heart.

Camilla's mom was sitting in the doorway.
Camilla approached her with ONE tear
sliding down her cheek.

- I've been looking for you, Camilla,
  where have you been?

- It's all the wind's fault because...

(Her mom ignored her
because she had something very important to say).

- Listen to me, Camilla: you are almost an adult now,
  and it's time for you to forget about
  wearing trousers and suspenders.

But when she saw the tear
running down Camilla's cheek,
her mom tried to comfort her:

- Don't cry.
  I've braided a strand of my mane into
  a long thread for you to wear.

Camilla, who lately had grown a lot,
stood on tiptoe and, without her trousers
and suspenders,
gave her mother a big, big hug.

And she posed and displayed her new self,
so her mother could get a good look at her,
wearing a ring,
a silver streak
a nice bow made of silk,
a ribbon as black as ink,
a string from a violin,
a boot lace fastened with a small pin,
a long thread which made her look smart,
and a very, very, very light heart.